To my daughter, Colleen, who helped me
imagine this story
—J.G.

To all the hard working, patient, inspiring
and dedicated teachers
—R.C.

First published in hardback in the USA by HarperCollins Publishers Inc. in 2009
First published in paperback in Great Britain by HarperCollins Children's Books in 2009

1 3 5 7 9 10 8 6 4 2
ISBN: 978-0-00-731878-0

Typography by Jeanne L. Hogle

Visit our website at: www.harpercollins.co.uk

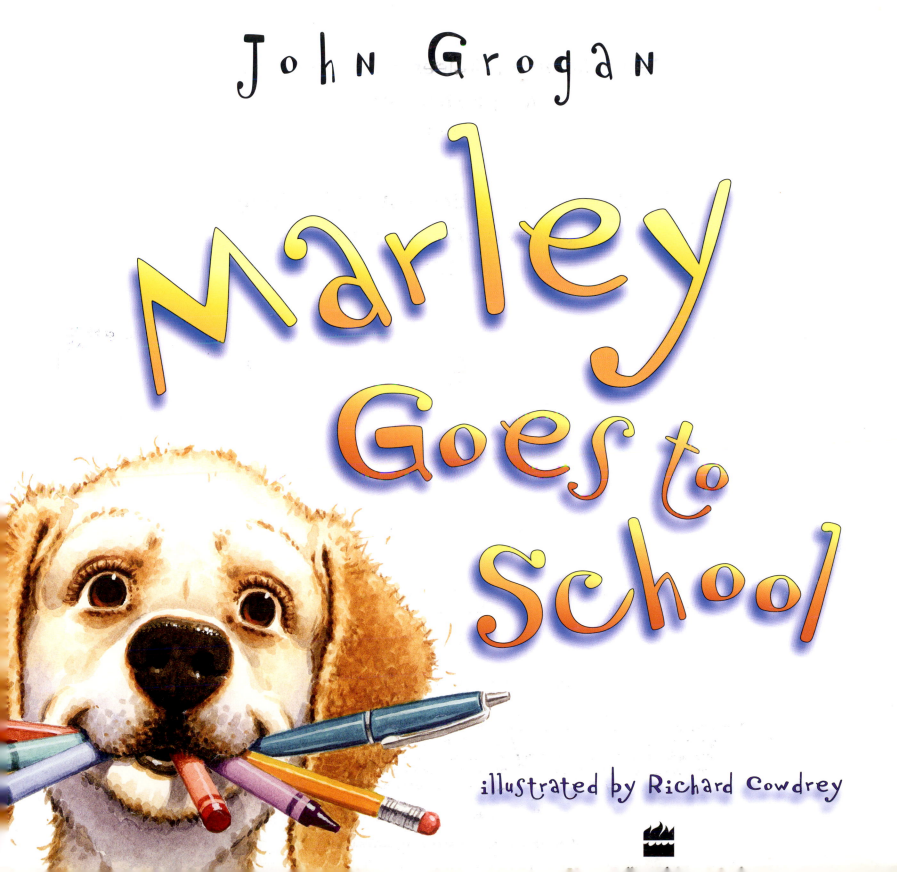

John Grogan

Marley
Goes to
School

illustrated by Richard Cowdrey

It was the first day of school and Cassie laid out her back-to-school supplies.

Pencils. Check.

Crayons. Check.

Ruler. Check.

Paper. Check.

Marley was all set for the big day too.

By the front door, he laid out his supplies.

Chewy bone. Arf!

Squeaky toy. Woof!

Liver treats. Ruff!

Favourite blanket. Awooo!

Baby Louie crawled around the corner. "Waddy go school too!" he exclaimed.

Mummy looked at Marley thumping his tail by the front door. "I don't think so, Big Boy," she said.

"I definitely don't think so," added Daddy.

"You silly dog," Cassie said, patting Marley on his big square head. "School's for children, not dogs."

Marley cocked his head and let out a low whine. Cassie was his best friend and he was used to going everywhere she went. To the park. To the playground. To Grandma's house.

Even to bed!

"Grab your backpack," Mummy called out. "We don't want to be late."

"Arf! Arf!" Marley said, grabbing his lead in his teeth and hopping up on his hind legs and dancing by the door.

"Arf! Arf! yourself," Mummy said. "You're going in the garden where you can't get into trouble."

"Good idea," said Daddy, and the whole family set off to walk Cassie to school.

Marley did not stay in the garden for long. He started to dig. And he dug and dug and dug. And the dirt flew up behind him until it formed a giant pile, a real Mount Marley. Up flew Mummy's marigolds. Out flopped Daddy's daffodils. Away went Cassie's carrot patch. Soon he had cleared a nice, cosy tunnel under the garden fence. With a wiggle and a waggle and a whip-whop of his tail, he belly-crawled to freedom.

Marley sniffed his way to the pavement, looked both ways – *All clear!* – and followed Cassie's scent straight to the front door of the school.

The front door was propped open. *They're expecting me!* Marley thought and he walked right in.

Down the corridor he trotted, stopping in each room in search of his beloved Cassie.

Marley tried the photocopying room. *Hmmm, not in here,*
he thought and then he took a moment to leave a calling card.

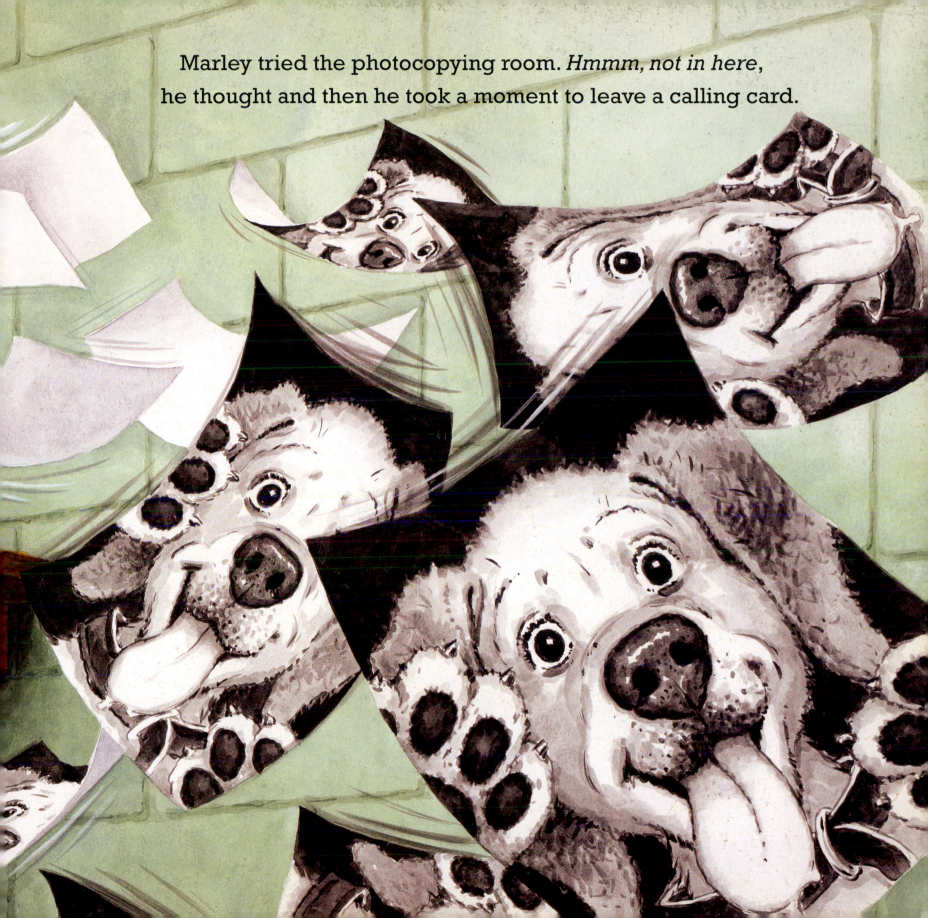

He tried the canteen, where the cooks were busy making lunch. He did not find Cassie, but Marley found the next best thing: a huge pile of juicy hot dogs. *Well, I don't mind if I do!*

"Hey! You're not supposed to be in here!" one of the dinner ladies yelled. "Shoo! Go home!"

"Burrrrp!" answered Marley. . .

. . . and he trotted over to the music room, where the orchestra was warming up. *Hmmm, she's not here either,* thought Marley, and then he joined the band for a song.

In the science lesson, Marley did not find Cassie, but he did find a cage with ten white mice inside. *What are you doing in there?* With a scratch of his paw and a flip of his nose, Marley opened the cage door and the mice scampered to freedom. He barked excitedly as if to ask, "Who wants to help me find Cassie?"

Marley followed the mice to the library, where the quiet didn't last long.

"Mice!" screamed a little girl.

"Big fat ones!" shouted a little boy.

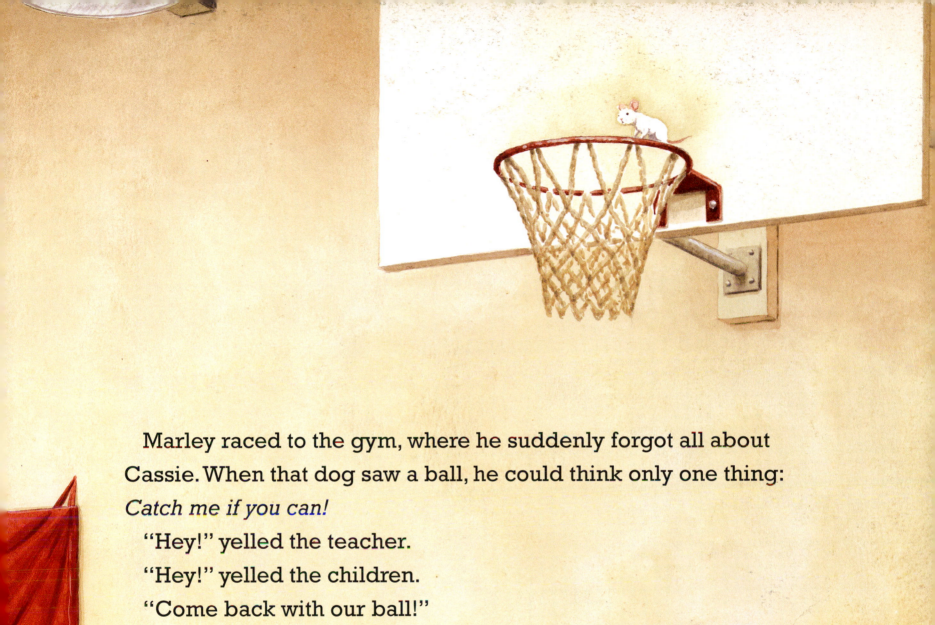

Marley raced to the gym, where he suddenly forgot all about Cassie. When that dog saw a ball, he could think only one thing: *Catch me if you can!*

"Hey!" yelled the teacher.

"Hey!" yelled the children.

"Come back with our ball!"

But Marley did not come back. He streaked down the hall, skidded around the corner, did a somersault and slid right into Mrs Weatherbee's maths lesson. Mrs Weatherbee peered through her thick glasses as she wrote on the blackboard.

"Oh my," she announced. "We've just received a report of a wild animal on the loose in our school. If you come across this animal, stay back. He may be dangerous."

"Yes, Mrs Weatherbee," the students said.

"Has anyone seen him?"

"No, Mrs Weatherbee," the students said.

But they had seen him. . .

. . . and helped make sure that Mrs Weatherbee would not. When the bell rang, Marley's ears pricked up. Outside, he heard the happy shrieks of children playing. There was no sound Marley loved more than the sound of children at play. He headed towards it.

"Not so fast, Naughty Boy." The voice came from behind him. Gulp! It was the headmistress, Mrs Peabody. She seized Marley by the collar and read his tag. "Aha! Cassie's dog. I should have known."

She tied Marley to the radiator with a rope. "Face the corner," she said. "I'm calling your parents."

But when Mrs Peabody returned two minutes later, all she found was half a rope, wet with dog drool. "Oh no!" she said.

"There he goes!" shouted the deputy headmaster, Mr Tanner. "He's heading to the playground!"

"I'll head him off," cried the gym teacher.

"I'm on his tail!" declared Mrs Weatherbee, shaking her fists.

"Tackle him!" screamed the dinner ladies.

The grown-ups chased Marley across the playground. They chased him through the tunnel and over the tyres and under the hoops. They chased him around the climbing frame and down the slide. They chased him under the swings and past the see-saw.

They chased him right into Cassie's arms.

"Marley!" Cassie shrieked with delight. "You did come to school!"

"Is that your dog?" Mr Tanner asked.

"Um," Cassie said. "He looks somewhat familiar."

"There you are!" Mummy and Daddy yelled.

"Bad dog, Marley!"

"Bah boo boo, Waddy!"

Baby Louie said.

"Now, now," said Mrs Peabody, "all's well that ends well." And Marley was so happy he jumped in the air and gave the headmistress a big, fat, sloppy kiss right on the lips.

Teacher's pet!

John Grogan's first book, *Marley & Me: Life and Love with the World's Worst Dog,* was first published in 2005 and rapidly became an international number 1 bestseller. It has now been adapted into the bestselling picture book *Bad Dog, Marley!* and bestselling junior memoir *MARLEY: A Dog Like No Other* and inspired its follow-up, *A Very Marley Christmas*. John is an award-winning newspaper columnist and former magazine editor. He lives with his wife and three children and their new dogs, Gracie (pictured) and Woodson in Pennsylvania, USA. You can visit him online at www.marleyandme.com.

Richard Cowdrey has illustrated numerous books for children. He lives in Ohio, USA, with his wife and children and their yellow Labrador, Murphy. You can visit him online at: www.rcowdrey.com.

The author *John Grogan*

© ADAM NADEL